JEWEL STICKER STORIES

A Dozen Easter Eggs

By Jennifer Dussling
Illustrated by Melissa Sweet

Grosset & Dunlap • New York

Copyright © 1997 by Grosset & Dunlap, Inc. Illustrations copyright © 1997 by Melissa Sweet.
All rights reserved. Published by Grosset & Dunlap, Inc., a member of The Putnam &
Grosset Group, New York. GROSSET & DUNLAP is a trademark of Grosset & Dunlap, Inc.
Published simultaneously in Canada. Printed in the U.S.A.

ISBN 0-448-41496-1   D E F G H I J

It was the day before Easter, and the Easter Bunny was getting everything ready. He straightened the bows on the Easter baskets, he fluffed up the pet chicks, and finally he counted the eggs. It was then that he made a terrible discovery. A dozen Easter eggs were missing!

The Easter Bunny pulled on his ears. "I have to find those Easter eggs by tomorrow," he said. "Maybe they rolled away into my bedroom." The Easter Bunny checked his bedroom. He found one pretty little Easter egg, but that was all.

Can you find the Easter egg?
Mark it with an Easter jewel.

"I'll look in the paint shop," said the Easter Bunny, tucking the egg into his basket. "Maybe some got left behind." The Easter Bunny went to the paint shop, and, sure enough, there was another Easter egg.

If you can find the egg, put a jewel on it.

Next the Easter Bunny looked in the basket room, where the bunnies were busy weaving.

"Have you seen any extra Easter eggs?" the Easter Bunny asked.

"No," they answered. "But take a look around."

Do you see the hidden egg?
Decorate it with a jewel.

With three eggs in his basket, the Easter Bunny went to the Jelly-beanery to look for more. And the Easter Bunny got lucky again. He discovered two painted eggs!

Mark each egg with an Easter jewel.

On the way to the flower garden, the Easter Bunny
thought about the missing eggs. They had not just rolled
away or been left behind. Someone had hidden them!
But who?

Do you see another egg? Put an Easter jewel on it.
And can you guess who hid it?

"Six down, six to go," said the Easter Bunny as he hopped into the chocolate room. This was where the chocolate bunnies for the Easter baskets were carved. Today the Easter Bunny hardly saw them. He was too excited, because he found another egg right away.

Find the hidden Easter egg
and decorate it with a jewel.

"Maybe there will be an egg by the pond," the Easter Bunny said to himself. He searched high and low and finally found another egg.

Can you find the egg? Put an
Easter jewel on it.

The Easter Bunny hurried to the hen house. He stuck his head inside and called out to the chickens, "Don't mind me. I'm not going to bother your nice white eggs. I'm just looking for painted ones!"

The Easter Bunny found the only Easter egg in the place.

Do you see the only painted egg?
Decorate it with an Easter jewel.

There was one last place to look—the room where the bunnies put a big ribbon on every last Easter basket.

The Easter Bunny found two more eggs there. He had found eleven Easter eggs! Almost the full dozen!

If you can find the two Easter eggs,
mark them with Easter jewels.

"Where could that last egg be?" the Easter Bunny asked, as he went back to put the eleven eggs with all the others. He pushed open the door and there, in the middle of the room, was a huge Easter basket with lots of chocolate bunnies and jelly beans, a big purple bow, and...the last Easter egg!

Decorate the Easter Bunny's Easter basket with lots of Easter jewels!

"Surprise!" said a voice in the corner. It was the littlest bunny of all. "You needed an Easter egg hunt of your own," he explained. "So I hid them all for you. Happy Easter, Easter Bunny!"